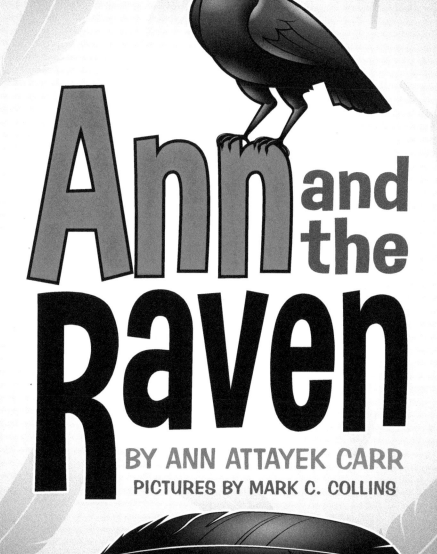

Ann and the Raven

BY ANN ATTAYEK CARR
PICTURES BY MARK C. COLLINS

THANK YOU POE!
I WILL ALWAYS LOVE YOU!

The Omnibus Publishing

5422 Ebenezer Rd., PO Box 152

Baltimore, MD 21162

www.theomnibuspublishing.com / info@omnibuspub.com

Ordering Information: Special discounts are available on quantity purchases by corporations, associations, and others. For details, contact the publisher at the address above.

Baltimore / Ann Attayek Carr — First Edition

ISBN 978-1-7335985-5-2 / Library of Congress Cataloging-In-Publication Data, Control Number Contact Publisher

Printed in the United States of America

Ann is very sad.

Very unusual things are
happening in the world.
People have to stay
inside of their homes.

Ann **HATES** staying inside.
She misses going to work.

She misses walking around
the harbor in Baltimore

Mostly she misses shopping for the coolest clothes at her favorite stores.

At night, Ann dreams about dressing up in
the perfect outfit and going out with her friends.

Since she can't walk outside,
Ann goes walking inside of
the huge garage next to
where she lives.

It goes up and up and up
and around and around.

But Ann is still sad and lonely.

Then **SOMETHING
AMAZING HAPPENS!**

One day during
Ann's walk in the
huge garage, she see's
a big black bird
sitting on the wall.

A BIG **BLACK** BIRD!

ANN **LOVES** BLACK!
IT'S HER
FAVORITE COLOR!

HOW COOL!

The big black bird is very close and does not move when Ann walks by. Until . . .

SUDDENLY the big black bird starts squawking VERY LOUDLY at Ann

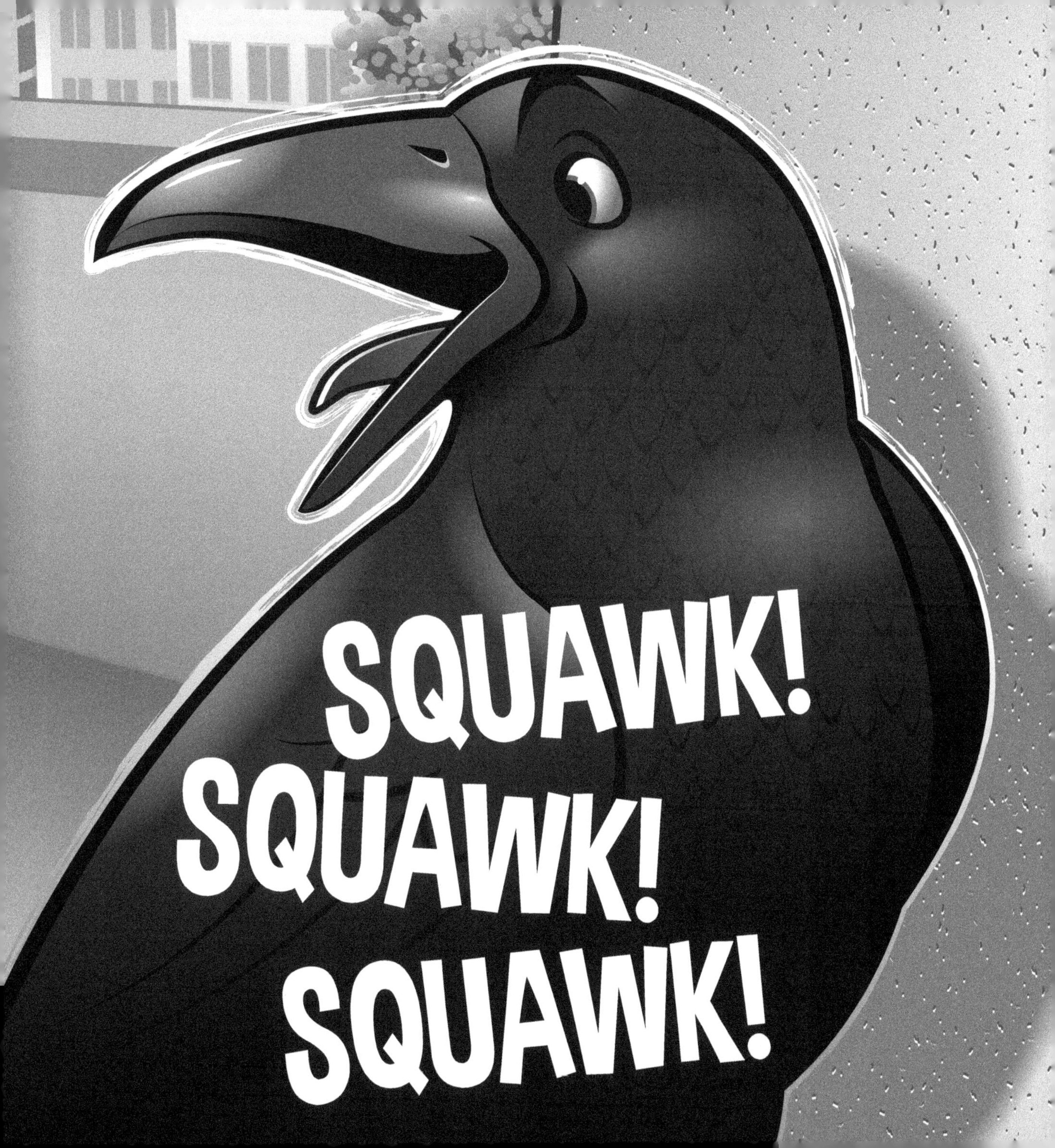
SQUAWK!
SQUAWK!
SQUAWK!

Ann thinks this is
EXTRA FUNNY!
ANN LOVES THIS
BIG BLACK BIRD!

Ann cannot stop smiling
as she walks away.

She feels like hopping up
and down with happiness!

Ann thinks about the big black bird when she's back inside.

"What kind of bird was that?"

Suddenly, she knows it was a Raven!
The Raven was **RAVING AT HER!**

E. A. POE

Ann decides to name the Raven **POE**
after a famous poet who lived in Baltimore.

Ann sees **POE** again, but he flies away.

"OH NO! OH NO!" thinks Ann.
"WHAT DID I DO WRONG?"

Ann thinks and thinks and thinks.
What can she do to see **POE** again?

Since people have to stay inside, maybe there are
fewer crumbs on the street for birds to eat.

Is **POE** hungry?

Is this why he was raving at her?

Ann leaves some bread for **POE**
the next time she goes for a walk.

Later **POE IS THERE**, but he is not perched near the bread.

POE watches quietly.

Ann walks away, then turns around to look.

POE has moved
and is **NOW EATING THE BREAD!**

Ann leaves bread and seeds
for **POE** every day.

Sometimes they see each other.

Sometimes they do not.

Ann understands.

She knows **POE** has a lot of
other things to do and places to go.

Sometimes **POE** visits Ann in her dreams.

A friend told Ann
that Ravens are the
bringers of magic.

And like magic, **POE** makes her
SMILE and **SMILE** and **SMILE**.

POE also gave Ann the idea
to write this book.

Ann always wanted to write a book!

THE END

First time children's book author, Ann Attayek Carr, has been a corporate level consultant, executive coach, student of classical piano, and Peace Corps volunteer.

As a Peace Corps volunteer in Kenya, she managed a women's business development enterprise. Later, she lead an international volunteer program for the American Red Cross. Outside of book writing, Ann has written and published several articles in the *Gestalt Review*. She is owner and principal of Intruequest®, an organizational effectiveness and executive coaching firm.

Her first book, "**Ann and the Raven**", is inspired by the true events she experienced during her time quarantined in the 2020 global pandemic. A self-proclaimed "wanna-be creative," Ann dreams of being a fashion designer when she grows up.

CPSIA information can be obtained
at www.ICGtesting.com
Printed in the USA
LVHW071045220121
677175LV00007B/356